RICHARD SCARRY'S
The Cat Family's Busy Day

A GOLDEN BOOK • NEW YORK
Western Publishing Company, Inc., Racine, Wisconsin 53404

Father Cat

lamp

Mother Cat

table

rug

closet

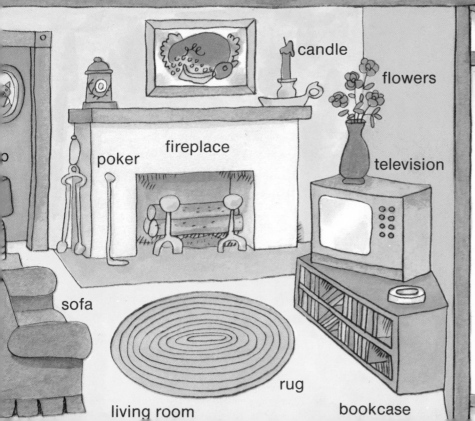

candle

flowers

fireplace

poker

television

sofa

rug

living room

bookcase

This is the Cat family's house.
There's Huckle Cat.
There's Sally Cat.
There's Father Cat and Mother Cat.
And also, in Huckle Cat's bedroom, there's Lowly Worm, a friend who lives with them.
Lowly likes to sleep late.

ladle

rolling pin

colander

spatula

carving knife

paring knife

saucepan

teakettle

Mother Cat

toast

frying pan

apron

toaster

sponge

faucet

Mother Cat is making breakfast
for Huckle. Sally has already
eaten.

sink

soap

dish

brush

strainer

measuring spoons

eggbeater

grater

bottle opener

wire whisk

scale

coffeepot

basket

teapot

glass

p and saucer

fork

plate

knife

spoon

butter

salt

pepper

tablecloth

keys

television

lamp

MARCH

calendar

broom

garbage can

record player

camera

books

bookcase

mop

soap

bucket

detergent

scrub brush

radio

thre.

buttons

thimble

Sally carries the mop.

telephone

pocket watch

vacuum cleaner

Father Cat vacuums the living room.

small mouse

Huckle empties the wastebasket.

After breakfast, everyone helps with the housework. Lowly helps clear the table. Be careful, Lowly.

wastebasket

sewing machine

needle

scissors

safety pin

tape measure

pincushion

Mother Cat is sewing.

school bus

SCHOOL BUS

compressor

roadblock

bug car

Cat family

The Cat family gets into the car and drives to town. They are going to pick up Grandma at the airport. She is coming to visit them.

mouse race car

pencil car

pea pod car for two

televi
truc

street repairman

pneumatic drill

bananamobile

small bug taxi

peanut car

fire fighter

fish truck

fire engine

lemonmobile

In Busytown, they meet
a lot of busy people.
Look at all the busy workers.
Oh, dear! There goes
Mr. Frumble's hat.

rug

tennis rack

key and padlock

tuba

life preserver

potted plant

mouse at work

hat

Mr. Frumble

umbrella

hot dog cart

HOT DOGS

golf clubs

plumber

guitar

sailor

clergyman

church

intbrush

papers

busy cat

Mr. Raccoon,
the construction worker

street cleaner

Mr. Fix-It

chef

And a busy cat has lost
all his papers.

bug bulldozer

tennis player

bug TV camera truck

Now the Cat family
passes by the beach.
But they do not have
time for a swim.

sun

sailboat

lighthouse

tent

waves

lunch

sand castle

surfer mouse

pail

shovel

starfish

lifeguard

DRINK WATER

blimp

hot dog stand

balloon

Big Hilda Hippo

stairs

umbrella

newspaper

crab playing with a ball

shell

oyster

scarecrow

scale

grocer

chicks

pumpkin

FRUITS

| lemon | apple | raspberry | cherry | grap |
| pear | melon | strawberry | plum | blue |

carrots

lettuce

The vegetable stand has lots of wonderful things.

flying watermelons

Sergeant Murphy

watermelon truck

ND VEGETABLES

es · peach · corn · cucumber · peas · lettuce · squash · tomato · beet

nge · pineapple · celery · radish · bean · cabbage · turnip · carrot · onion

asparagus

potatoes

watermelon

peanuts

cornmobile

Cat family

small pencil car

Do you know the names
of all of them?

asphalt spreader

Oh, dear! Mr. Frumble has done it again.
He's hit a dump truck.

dump truck

line painter

steamroller

fresh asphalt

furious engineer

small concrete buggy

You really must be careful,
Mr. Frumble.

lying down

reading

kneeling

dancing

digging

watering

running

pushing

riding

pulling

talking

smiling

eating and drinking

singing and dancing

It's recess at school.
What things do you see the pigs doing?

kicking

falling

crying

frowning

lighthouse keeper

And in the busy harbor,
a lot of things are happening.
What do you see happening?

lighthouse

fishing net

speedboat

sinking boat

fishing boat

car ferry

oars

rubber raft

wharf

life jacket

boat on fire

fire fighter

fireboat

small fishing boat

lifeboat

Coast Guard boat

bell buoy

captain

life preserver

flag

fisherman

cabin cruiser

tail

propeller plane

sun

jet plane

flight attendant

cabin windows

wing

jet engines

Finally they arrive at the airport.
Grandma's plane has just landed.

baggage handler

biplane

Cat family

mouse pilot

Everyone is so happy.
Grandma is sure to enjoy her visit.

TV reporter

baggage train